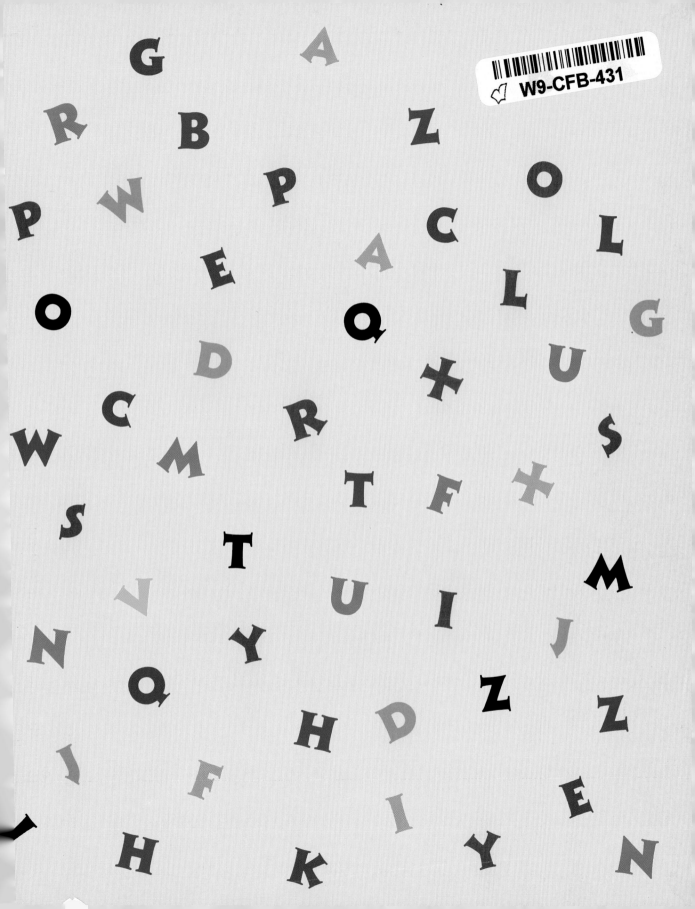

Dear Imagination Library Graduate,

My, how time flies. It seems it was only yesterday when your family and friends read you your first story. You were just a baby. Now you're five years old and about to go to school. How exciting!

This may be your last book from my Imagination Library but you have to promise me you will keep on reading. Every book is a treasure and every time you open one up you will meet new friends and take wonderful journeys to magical places.

I hope you have a great time in school. You and all of your friends are very special. There is no limit to what you can do or how far you can go. Just remember the lessons my family taught me - dream big dreams; learn everything you can learn; and care for all of those who care for you. You do all of these things and you can be anyone you want to be.

You are terrific and remember...

I Will Always Love You,

Dolly

Miss Bindergarten

Gets Ready for Kindergarten

by **JOSEPH SLATE**

illustrated by **ASHLEY WOLFF**

Dutton Children's Books · New York

Library of Congress Cataloging-in-Publication Data
Slate, Joseph.   Miss Bindergarten gets ready for kindergarten/by Joseph Slate; illustrated by Ashley Wolff.—1st ed.   p.   cm.
Summary: Introduces the letters of the alphabet as Miss Bindergarten and her students get ready for kindergarten.
Special Markets ISBN-13 978-0-525-47925-3, ISBN-10 0-525-47925-2 Not for Resale
[1. Alphabet.   2. Animals—Fiction.   3. Kindergarten—Fiction.   4. Schools—Fiction.   5. Stories in rhyme.]   I. Title.
PZ8.3.S629Mi   1996   [E]—dc20   96-14692   CIP   AC

Published in the United States 1996 by Dutton Children's Books, a division of Penguin Young Readers Group
345 Hudson Street, New York, New York 10014
Designed by Semadar Megged · Manufactured in China · First Edition · 25 24 23 22

To Maureen Sheridan Johnson
and all the other Miss Bindergartens,
wherever you are —J.S.

For Margy and Bill,
two of my favorite teachers —A.W.

It is the first day
of kindergarten,
and—
oh, oh, oh!—

Adam Krupp
wakes up.

Brenda Heath brushes her teeth.

Christopher Beaker finds his sneaker.

Miss Bindergarten gets ready for kindergarten.

Danny Hess
rushes to dress.

Emily Moko
cools her cocoa.

Fran Lister
kisses her sister.

Miss Bindergarten gets ready for kindergarten.

Gwen McGunny
packs her bunny.

Henry Fetter

fights his sweater.

Ian Lowe says, "I won't go!"

Miss Bindergarten gets ready for kindergarten.

Jessie Sike
pedals her bike.

Kiki Wong
hops along.

Lenny Loome says, "Vroo-vroo-vrooom!"

Miss Bindergarten gets ready for kindergarten.

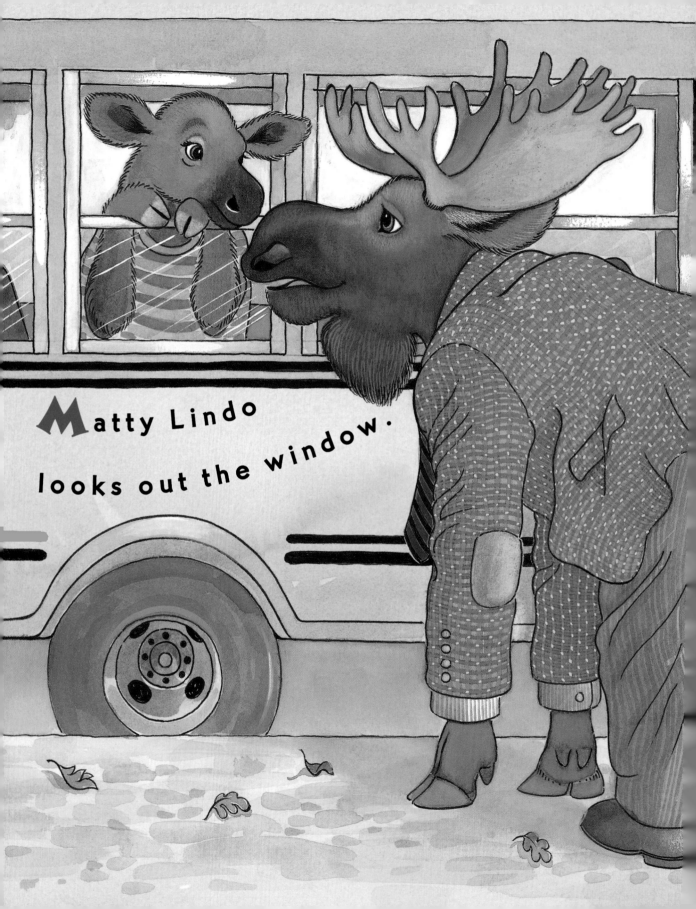

Matty Lindo looks out the window.

Ophelia Nye hugs good-bye.

Noah Bonn climbs right on.

Miss Bindergarten gets ready for kindergarten.

Patricia Packer sneaks a cracker.

Quentin Wend high-fives his friend.

Miss Bindergarten is *almost* ready

for kindergarten.

Tommy Tuttle jumps a puddle.

Vicky Densel

bites her pencil.

Ursula Crewe

ties her shoe.

Now Miss Bindergarten is all ready

for kindergarten.

Wanda Chin
marches in.

Xavier Roe
yells
"Hello!"

Yolanda Pound looks around.

Zach Blair finds his chair.

"Good morning, kindergarten,"

says Miss Bindergarten.

And—oh, oh, oh!—

the fun's begun!

Adam · Alligator

Brenda · Beaver

Christopher · Cat

Danny · Dog

Emily · Elephant

Fran · Frog

Gwen · Gorilla

Henry · Hippopotamus

Ian · Iguana

Jessie · Jaguar

Kiki · Kangaroo

Lenny · Lion

Matty · Moose

Noah · Newt

Ophelia · Otter

Patricia · Pig

Quentin · Quokka

Raffie · Rhinoceros

Sara · Squirrel

Tommy · Tiger

Ursula · Uakari monkey

Vicky · Vole

Wanda · Wolf

Xavier · Xenosaurus

Yolanda · Yak

Zach · Zebra

Coco · Cockatoo